ARANEA

A Story About A Spider

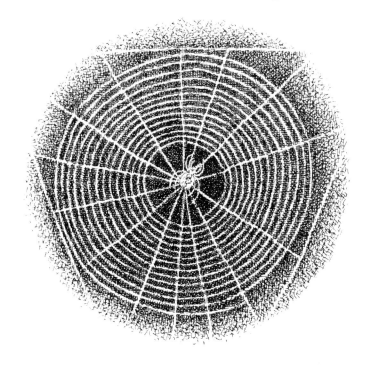

Story by Jenny Wagner   Illustrations by Ron Brooks

c 1975   no p. il. $6.95
0-87888-138-7
78-55212

Bradbury Press   Scarsdale, New York

Library of Congress Cataloging in Publication Data
Wagner, Jenny. Aranea: a story about a spider.
Summary: An industrious spider spends her days and nights
spinning perfect webs.
[1. Spiders–Fiction] I. Brooks, Ron. II. Title.
PZ7.W12425Ar [E] 78-55212
ISBN 0-87888-138-7

ARANEA

A Story About A Spider

Aranea stood in the wind, spinning and spinning.

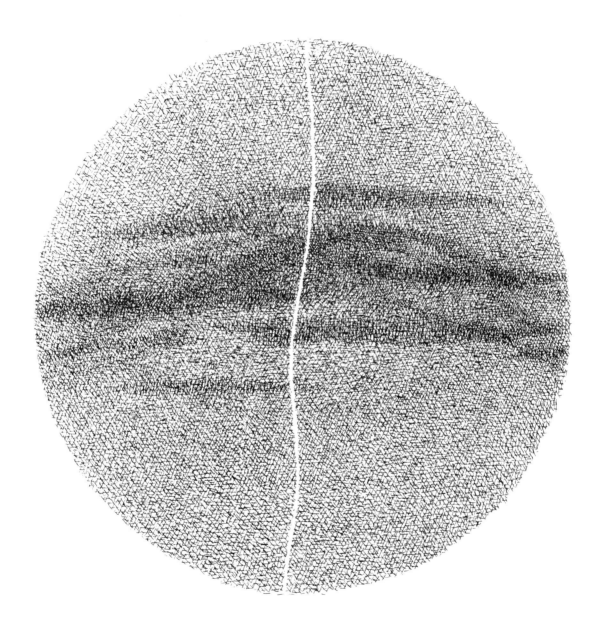

A fine silk thread lifting into the air and hanging there, caught on the wind.

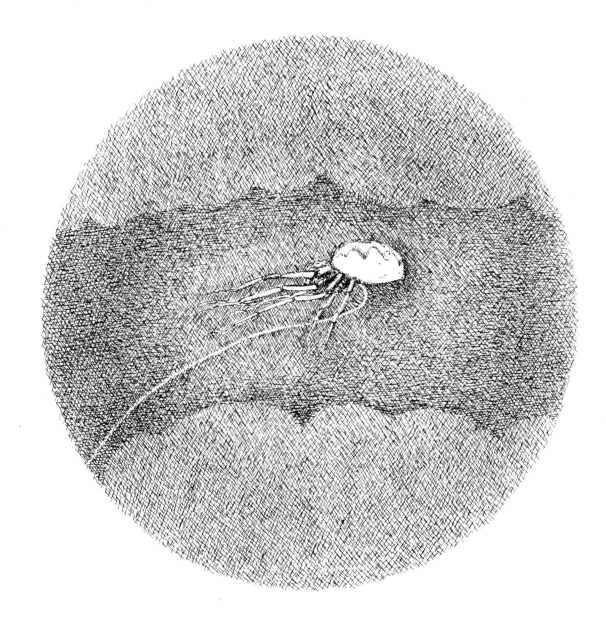

The wind lifted it up; Aranea clung to her thread and floated with it.

For a whole day she swung in the wind,
swinging and blowing wherever it took her.

Then she landed on a lilac bush in somebody's garden.

She crawled into the curl of a leaf and made herself a hiding place, and waited.

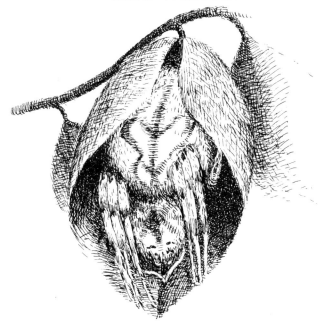

At dusk she crept out and made her first web.

First the cross piece   then the frame

then round and round the long spiral   until it was perfect.

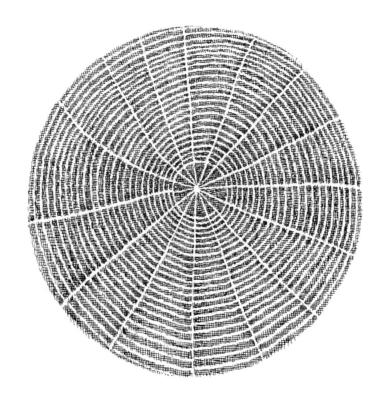

In the morning the web was still there, but only for a little while.
Early, before many people were out of doors, Aranea
tore it down so that no one would see it.

Then she hid in the curl of her leaf and waited till dusk.

Through many still summer days and nights Aranea
built her web and broke it again.
Few people saw it, or even knew she was there.

Sometimes, very early, when the boys were going to school, they saw it.

she felt the fine silk threads on her face, and said, 'Ugh! A spider's web!'

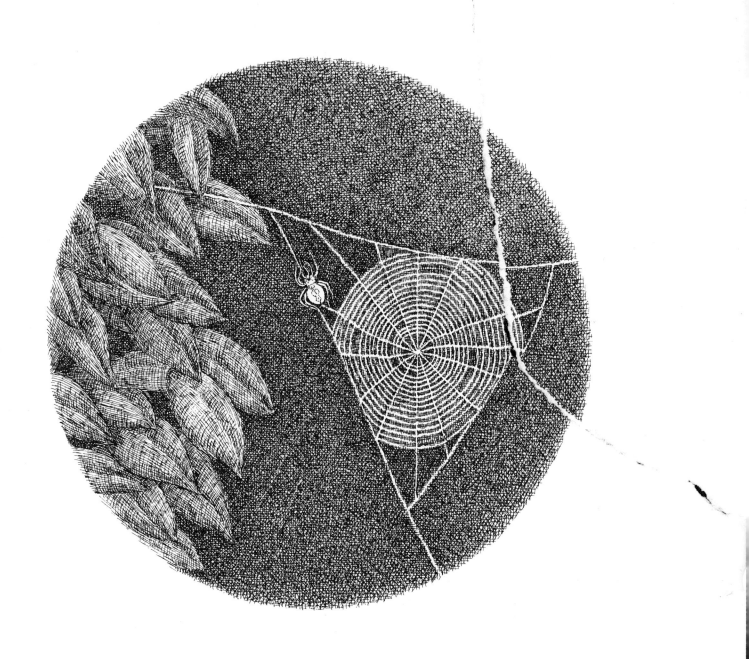

But no one ever saw Aranea.

Until one night, near the end of summer.

Sometimes when their mother was hanging out the clothes

And they swished sticks through it and broke it.

Aranea knew that night there was something wrong.
The cross piece for the web would not catch properly;
again and again she threw it out,
but the air was damp and heavy,
and the thread would not lift.
She made the web as well as she could,
but it was not perfect.
Then she curled in her leaf and waited.

The sky turned black, but no stars came out.
There was no moon.
Everything was very still and very quiet.
Presently a wind came up and Aranea felt the line sway under her feet.
The wind grew stronger,
and a piece of the frame came loose.
Aranea tried to mend it,
but the wind tore it away.
The lilac bush shook,
and the trees in the garden rattled and hissed.

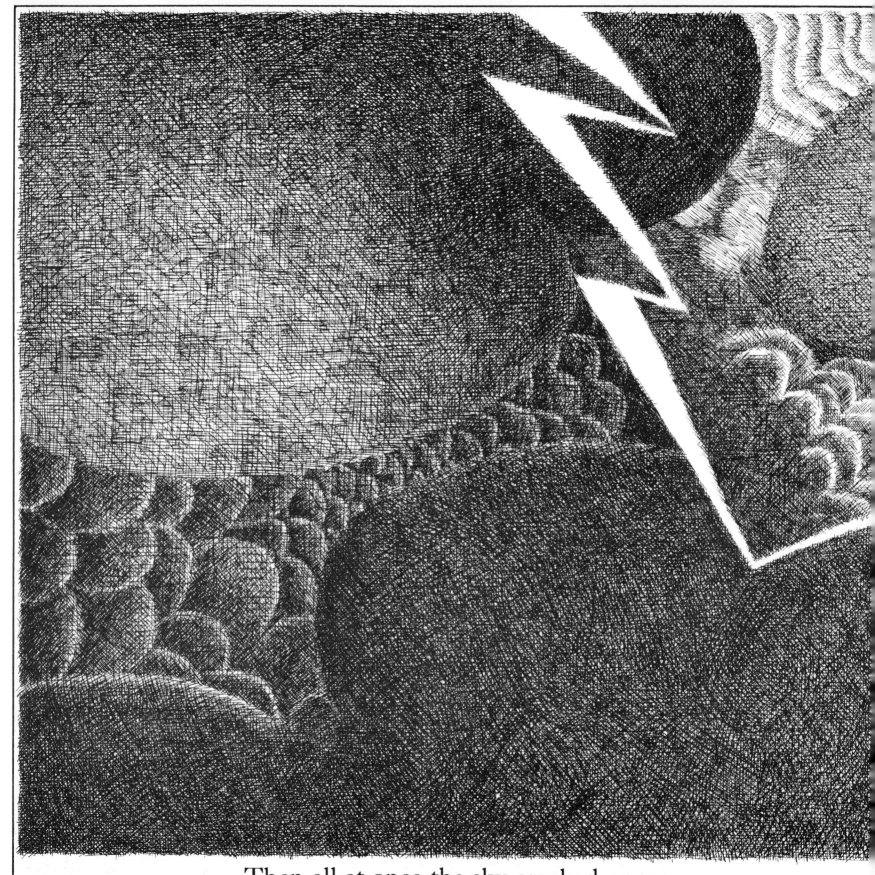

Then all at once the sky cracked open.

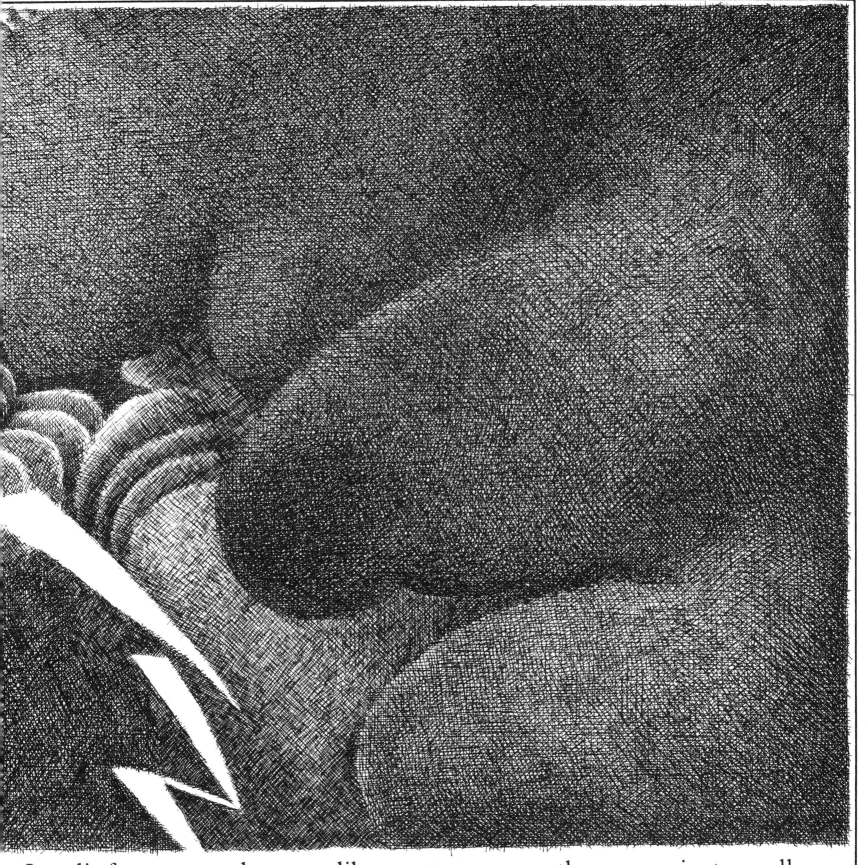

It split from top to bottom, like a rotten orange thrown against a wall.

For a moment the garden lit up like day.

Then the rain came down.

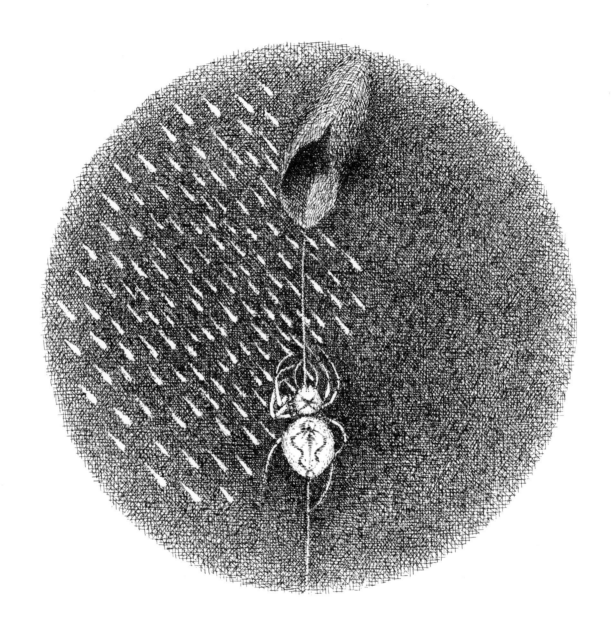

Aranea ran for her leaf, but the rain blocked her way.
It poured down steadily and heavily,
knocking her over which ever way she ran.

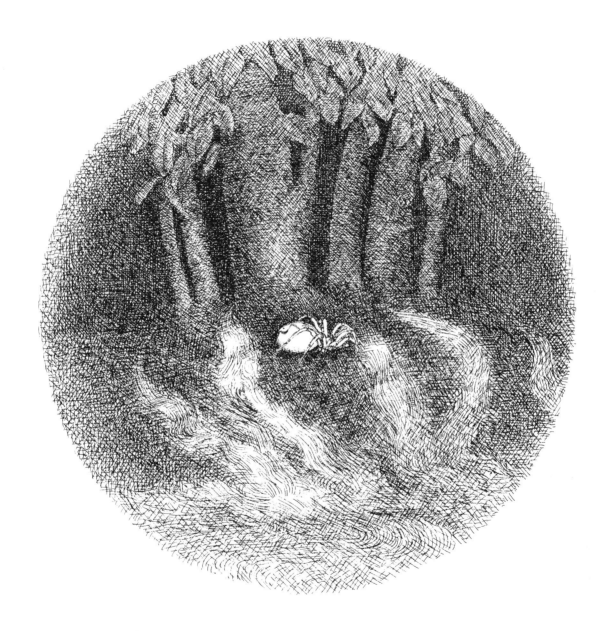

She dropped to the ground and crawled under the bush,
but there were streams of water there, too, running every way.
She clung to her line for a moment, trying to climb up for shelter;
then she found herself in the fast-running water
with the thread floating, useless, behind her.

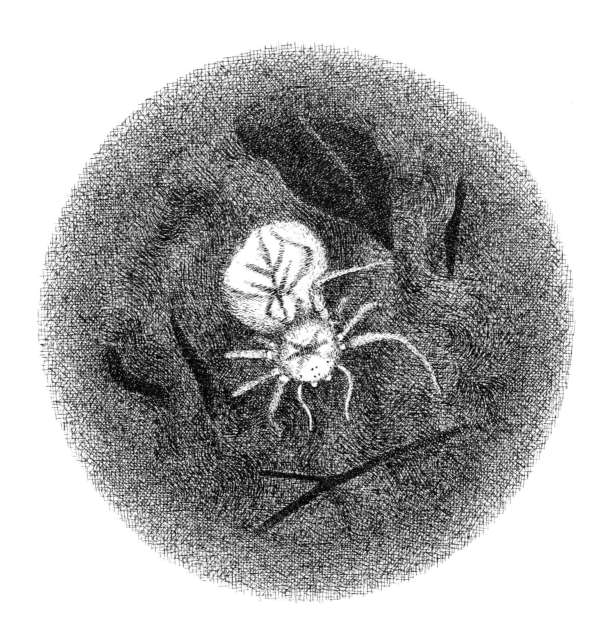

There were sticks in the water, and blades of grass, and leaves
and Aranea caught at each of them in turn without finding help.
Then the water slowed down and spread out.

Aranea crawled on to the back step of the house.

She rested there for a while,
and when she felt strong enough she crawled a little higher.
She crept under the crack of the door and into the house.

She climbed up and up, looking for a corner to hide in.

Suddenly everything was white.
Aranea clung to the wall and did not move.
The dark corners were gone; there was nothing but smooth white wall.

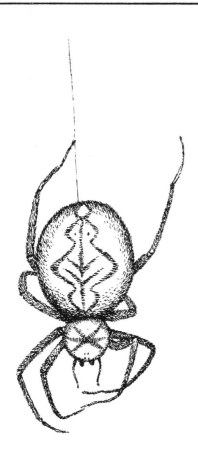

She climbed a little higher, and waited for a moment;
then she fastened her line and dropped.

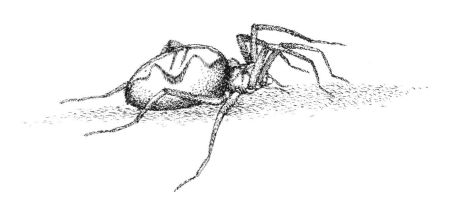

She ran over the floor and into the shadows;
and then she crawled into the laundry.

She found herself a safe dark hiding place, and waited.
She waited all that night, and all the next day.
And at dusk she crept into the garden.

She found the lilac bush, and her curling leaf
with the lining of silk she had made for it.
She pulled the edges more tightly together, and spread more silk inside.
Then she crept out and made her web.

First the cross piece

then the frame

then round and round the long spiral.

Until it was perfect.

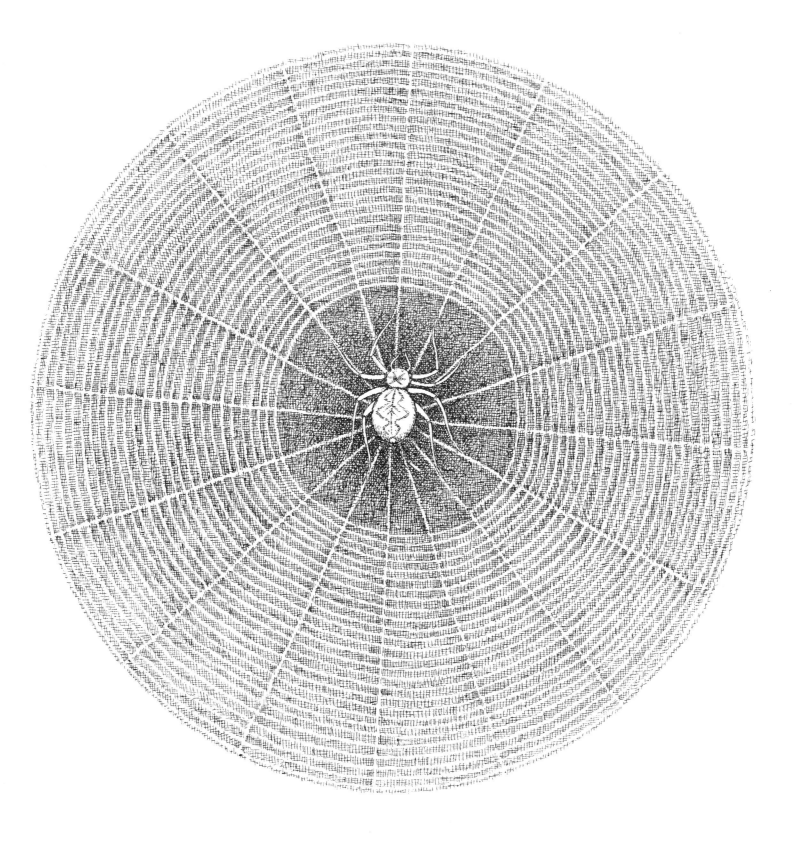